Ahoyty-Toyty

Ahoyty-Toyty

Helen Stephens

Picture Corgi Books

To Pop - the original handsome Captain.

AHOYTY-TOYTY
A PICTURE CORGI BOOK 0 552 54979 7

First published in Great Britain by David Fickling Books,
an imprint of Random House Children's Books

David Fickling edition published 2003
Picture Corgi edition published 2004

1 3 5 7 9 10 8 6 4 2

Copyright © Helen Stephens, 2003

Set in Bodoni MT

Corgi Books are published by Random House Children's Books,
61–63 Uxbridge Road, London W5 5SA,
a division of The Random House Group Ltd,
in Australia by Random House Australia (Pty) Ltd,
20 Alfred Street, Milsons Point, Sydney, NSW 2061, Australia,
in New Zealand by Random House New Zealand Ltd,
18 Poland Road, Glenfield, Auckland 10, New Zealand,
and in South Africa by Random House (Pty) Ltd,
Endulini, 5A Jubilee Road, Parktown 2193, South Africa

THE RANDOM HOUSE GROUP Limited Reg. No. 954009
www.kidsatrandomhouse.co.uk

A CIP catalogue record for this book is available from the British Library.

Printed in China

Victor is a well behaved, lovable pup and he lives with *Miss Loopy*. **Butch** is cool and bad and he lives with *Miss Froopy-Frou-Frou*.

Victor and **Butch** love holidays and this holiday was extra exciting because it was on a really big ship. **Victor** and **Butch** couldn't wait to explore.

They sniffed out the kitchens,

crept into the cabins,

wriggled through the portholes,

ran round the deck,

and leapt on to the ladies' laps.

Suddenly the Captain arrived.
"Ahoyty-toyty ladies," said
the Captain.

"Ahoyty-toyty Captain," giggled *Miss Loopy* and *Miss Froopy-Frou-Frou*.

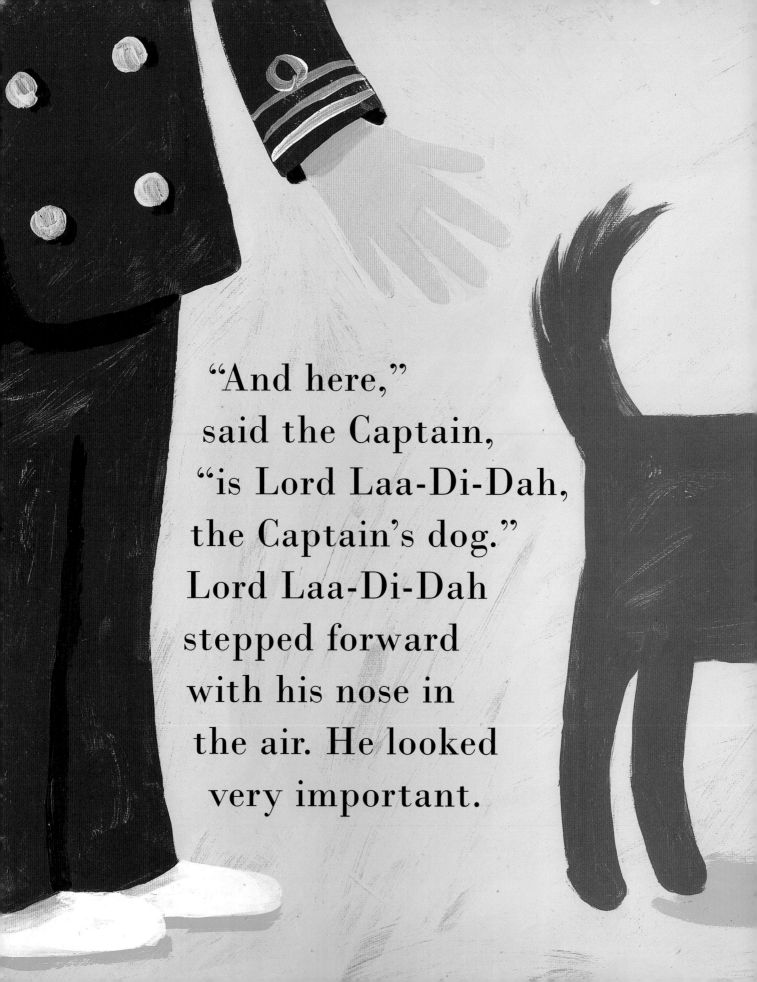

"And here,"
said the Captain,
"is Lord Laa-Di-Dah,
the Captain's dog."
Lord Laa-Di-Dah
stepped forward
with his nose in
the air. He looked
very important.

"Look at him!"
said **Butch**.
"He's fantastic!"

"Did you see how he walked with his nose in the air?" said **Butch**. "Let's practise walking like Lord Laa-Di-Dah."

"Is this right?"
said **Victor**.
"No," said **Butch**,
"it's like this."

Later **Butch** and **Victor**
saw Lord Laa-Di-Dah again.

He walked past
a pretty poodle
and he flashed her
a charming smile.
"Did you see that?"
said **Butch**.

"Let's practise our charming smiles, **Victor**," said **Butch**. "How's this?" said **Victor**. "No," said **Butch**. "It's like this."

Later they saw Lord
Laa-Di-Dah greet two
fluffy terriers.
"Ahoyty-toyty!"
said Lord Laa-Di-Dah.

"Did you hear that?" said **Butch**.
"Let's go up and say 'Ahoyty-toyty'
to Lord Laa-di-dah."
"Okay," said **Victor**.

"Ahoyty-toyty Lord Laa-Di-Dah," said **Butch**.

But **Victor** got muddled.
"Asployty-bloyty!" he said.
Lord Laa-Di-Dah looked
right down his nose
at **Victor.**

"You're a useless
Captain's dog!"
said **Butch.**

Just before
bedtime an
invitation
arrived.

"Where's my invitation?"
said **Victor**.
But **Victor** hadn't been invited.
"Don't worry Victor darling,"
said *Miss Loopy*.
"You can sit
with me and
*Miss Froopy-
Frou-Frou*."

The next evening **Butch** walked into the dining room with his nose in the air. He was wearing a bow tie and doing his best charming smile.

Butch sat at the Captain's table and waited.

But after a while his bow
tie began to itch, his face
ached from the charming
smile and he didn't really
like the posh nosh at the
Captain's table.

Still he waited.
He looked over at **Victor**
having a lovely time.
Butch felt miserable.

"Ahoyty-toyty," said
Lord Laa-Di-Dah
as he sat down.

"Asployty-bloyty-splithery-sployty and stick it up your snoyty!" shouted **Butch**. Then he ran straight over to his friend **Victor's** table.

"Any sausages left?"
said **Butch**.
"I saved you one,"
said **Victor**.

"Ahoyty-toyty
Victor," said
Butch.
"Asployty-bloyty
Butch,"
said **Victor**.